DANCES WITH WOLVES

Dances With Wolves: A Story for Children adapted by James Howe
from the screenplay by Michael Blake, based on his novel.
Copyright © 1991 by Tig Productions, Inc.

This book published simultaneously in the United States of America and in Canada, by Newmarket Press.

91 92 93 94   10 9 8 76 5 4 3 2 1

Library of Congress Cataloguing-in Publication Data
Howe, James, 1946–
Dances with wolves : a story for children / adapted by James Howe from the
screenplay by Michael Blake, based on his novel.
p. cm.
Summary: A Civil War army officer is sent west and becomes deeply involved in the affairs of an Indian
tribe.
ISBN 1-55704-104-0
1. Indians of North America—Juvenile fiction. [1. Indians of North America—Fiction. 2. West (U.S.)—
Fiction.] I. Dances with wolves (Motion picture). II. Title.
PZ7.H83727Dan   1991
[Fic]—dc20   91-20283
                                                                                                                   CIP
                                                                                                                    AC

Quantity Purchases
Companies, professional groups, clubs, and other organizations may qualify for special terms when ordering
quantities of this title. For information, write Special Sales, Newmarket Press, 18 East 48th Street. New York,
N.Y. 10017, or call (212) 832-3575.

Manufactured in the United States of America
Book Design by Tania Garcia

DANCES WITH WOLVES

A STORY FOR CHILDREN

ADAPTED BY **JAMES HOWE**
FROM THE SCREENPLAY BY **MICHAEL BLAKE** BASED ON HIS NOVEL
PHOTOGRAPHS BY **BEN GLASS**

NEWMARKET PRESS
NEW YORK

In the time when the buffalo ran free and the yellow prairie grass met the blue sky in four directions, a man came west. A white man so pale the Indians first called him The Man Who Shines Like Snow, he was a soldier who longed to see the frontier before it was gone. With his sturdy buckskin horse Cisco he rode deep into the Dakota Territory until he reached the westernmost post of the Union army. What he found was less than he'd hoped for and more than he'd ever dreamed. ✢

ᨃᨃᨃᨃᨃ FORT SEDGEWICK, 1864 ᨃᨃᨃᨃᨃ

The last thing Lieutenant Dunbar expected was a ghost town, yet a ghost town was what Fort Sedgewick most resembled. He could have turned back, but he was a soldier and this was his post.

As he unloaded the supplies he'd brought with him, he wondered what had happened to Captain Cargill and the men who were supposed to be stationed here. He had no way of knowing that only days earlier they had abandoned the fort, desperate after many months of waiting in vain for supplies and fresh troops.

Have arrived to find Fort Sedgewick deserted, he wrote in his journal that first night. *Am now waiting for garri-*

son's return or word from headquarters.

He rested his head against the wall of the sod hut he assumed had been Captain Cargill's quarters. It would be his now, at least until the captain returned. There were only two buildings in the entire fort: this one and a rundown supply hut.

The post is in exceedingly poor condition, he wrote, *and I have decided to assign myself clean-up duty beginning tomorrow.*

He laid his pen aside. Thinking of tomorrow put yesterday in his mind and the day before that and all the days that had brought him to this moment. It seemed impossible that only a handful of months earlier he had been fighting in the bloody Civil War back east. If he closed his eyes, he could still hear the yammering of the rifles and the cries of men in battle.

He heard his own cry among them, distinct but made distant by memory as if it now belonged to someone else. He had been a hero in that war. The cost had been pain and blood, but as a reward for his valor he had been given the choice of any post away from the front lines that he desired.

To the surprise of everyone but himself, he had asked to be posted on the frontier and his request had been granted.

Now, in the short time he'd been here, an incredible thing had occurred. He had fallen in love with the prairie. It didn't matter to him that he was alone, more alone than he'd ever been or felt in his entire life. The land itself was a companion.

He wrote, *Supplies are abundant, and the country is everything I dreamed it would be. There can be no place like this on earth.* He signed his name, *Lieutenant John J. Dunbar, U.S.A.,* and closed the book.

Even if Captain Cargill and his men never came back, he told himself, he was sure to hear from headquarters soon.

He did not know that the wagoneer who had brought him to Fort Sedgewick would be ambushed by a fierce band of Pawnee on his return to headquarters. Before the next moon rose in the Dakota skies, the last man on earth who knew of Dunbar's whereabouts would be dead.

Sleep did not come easy that night. Every little noise in the darkness asked for an explanation that Dunbar could not provide. He had heard stories about the wild Indians who lived in the West and now his mind was filled with images of painted savages with feathered heads and raised tomahawks. And yet ...

He could not deny he was eager to see them. They were part of it all, this adventure, his reason for being here. When at last he fell asleep, a strange sort of peace came over him. He couldn't explain it then, but later he would understand that despite his fears there was something about this place that calmed him. It was as if he had been wandering his whole life and he had finally come home.

✦ ✦ ✦

The days passed more quickly than he'd imagined they would. There was much to do. The broken-down corral needed mending, the quarters needed cleaning and repair, the supplies had to be stacked. A nearby river, his only source of water, had

been used as a dump by the soldiers who had lived on the fort before. Cleaning it out was not a pleasant task, but Dunbar was grateful for any activity that kept his mind from thinking about the Indians and wondering when he would hear from headquarters.

One day while working, Dunbar spotted something moving in the grass on the opposite side of the river. Instinctively, he raised his rifle. When he saw that it was a wolf, he thought perhaps he should be frightened but he wasn't. The animal didn't seem threatening or hungry, merely curious. He lowered his gun and the two of them stared at each other for a long time.

The wolf returned for several days. The lieutenant wrote in his journal, *There is a wolf who is intent on the goings on here. He has milky white socks on his front feet. If he comes calling tomorrow, I will name him Two Socks.*

The wolf did come calling and though he kept a distance Two Socks joined Cisco as Dunbar's only companions.

✦ ✦ ✦

Almost thirty days went by and there was still no sign of Cargill's command nor word from headquarters. Dunbar debated whether or not to go in search of the missing soldiers, but decided he should not abandon his post. He began instead to settle into a contented routine.

"Soldier, oh, soldier, won't you marry me
Before the fight comes home?
How can I marry a pretty little girl
When I got no shoes to put on?"

Dunbar sang happily as he scrubbed his clothes in the river. Naked, he felt at one with the clear water and the prairie grass, the sky and the buzzing insects. It was hard to imagine a better life.

Over the rise, out of his line of vision, someone was gazing thoughtfully at the changes in the army post: the tidy grounds, the great awning that had been added to the little sod hut, the repaired corral. The beautiful buckskin inside it.

The Indian who watched was named Kicking Bird. He was puzzled by what he saw. Before he and the other Sioux in Ten Bears' band had left these parts for their winter camping grounds, the fort had been a shambles, occupied by a small, tattered group of soldiers. The Indians had been careful to keep their distance and had remained undetected. Now that they were back at their summer camp eight miles down the river, Kicking Bird had returned to the fort to see for himself what the soldiers' fate had been.

What was before his eyes now was a mystery. It appeared that there was life here, but not the life of many — only a few, perhaps only one. What interested him most, however, was the horse. He had never seen a buckskin quite like it. He drew closer to take a better look.

Dunbar left his clothes to dry in the sun and climbed the bluff back to the fort. He was still singing when the music stuck in his throat and he threw himself on the ground. Someone was walking around the fort.

His heart pounded in his ears as he saw

the picture in his mind of just who that someone was. An Indian.

Slowly, he pulled himself up to peer over the top of the ridge. He watched as Kicking Bird entered the corral. The Indian approached Cisco with a rope in his hand. Dunbar was certain his horse was about to be stolen if he didn't do something.

Without thinking, he jumped up. "You there!" he cried.

Kicking Bird turned, startled by the sound and the sight of the naked white man walking rapidly toward him, glistening in the sun. Who was this creature with the skin that blinded the eyes? A god, perhaps. Staggering back, Kicking Bird turned to run and tore through the corral fence as if it were made of twigs. He leaped onto his pony and galloped away.

Stunned, Dunbar watched him go. It was only after the Indian was no longer in sight that he looked down and noticed, to his embarrassment, that he was naked.

That night, he drew a picture of the Indian in his journal, and he wrote, *Have made first contact with an Indian. I don't know how many there are, but where there's one, there's another.*

The next day, Dunbar outfitted his hut with rifles and extra provisions. He then buried all the excess weapons on the fort in a carefully hidden spot for fear that they would fall into enemy hands. As he marked the spot with a buffalo bone, he reflected that when

the Indians returned, he would be ready.

Cannot mount an adequate defense, he wrote, *but will try to make a big impression when they come. Waiting.*

Postscript.
The man I encountered was a magnificent-looking fellow.

THE VILLAGE ON THE RIVER

Soon after Kicking Bird's return to his village on the river, a council of warriors met in the tipi of their chief, Ten Bears. Ten Bears had long ago learned that the tongue of a chief speaks wisely only after his ears have listened wisely. He listened now as the others argued the case of the lone soldier Kicking Bird had discovered at the fort.

"I do not care for this talk about a white man!"

Several heads nodded in agreement at the angry words spoken by the warrior Wind In His Hair.

"Whatever he is, he is not a Sioux and that makes him less. When I hear that more whites are coming, I want to laugh. They don't ride well. They don't shoot well. They're dirty."

More heads nodded.

"These soldiers could not even make it through one winter here," Wind In His Hair went on. His voice grew stronger with his passion. "And these people are said to flourish? I think they will all be dead soon." He hesitated a moment, then added, as if it were a joke, "This fool is probably lost."

Wind In His Hair sat down as the Indians around him laughed.

Kicking Bird raised his hand, palm out.

"Wind In His Hair's words are strong," he said calmly, "and I have heard them. But make no mistake. The whites are coming. Even our enemies agree on this. So when I see one man alone without fear in our country I do not think he is lost. I think he may have medicine. I see someone who might speak for all the white people who are coming."

There were murmurs as the others considered the words Kicking Bird had spoken. To the Sioux, medicine meant that which could not be explained. It was a word implying something between mysterious and holy. Kicking

◇◇◇◇◇◇ *Ten Bears* ◇◇◇◇◇◇

Bird was the medicine man of his band. That he considered another — a white man, especially — to possess medicine was an assertion not to be taken lightly.

At last, Wind In His Hair spoke again. "Kicking Bird is always looking ahead and that is good. But this man is nothing to us. I will take some men.

We will shoot some arrows into this white man. If he truly has medicine, he will not be hurt. If he has no medicine, he will be dead."

To many, this seemed a good idea. But Ten Bears was wary of Wind In His Hair's hot temper. He knew that when one white man was killed, more were sure to come. He decided it would be best to take no action just yet.

"We should talk about this some more," he said. "That is all I have to say." And the meeting was over.

Wind In His Hair returned to his tipi, not happy with Ten Bear's decision. Since it was the way of the Sioux that any warrior could do as he pleased, he vowed he would take some action. Perhaps he would not shoot arrows into this white man who might be a god. But he would do something.

✢ ✢ ✢

It was Two Socks who first gave the warning. The lieutenant looked up from the river where he had come for his morning shave. He saw the look in the old wolf's eyes as they stared off at something he couldn't see.

In the distance, he heard hoofbeats.

Dunbar lay down his razor and put his hand to the big revolver and gunbelt that were slung over his shoulder. He

︿◦︿◦︿ *Wind In His Hair* ︿◦︿◦︿

moved toward the fort, slowly at first. When he looked back and saw that Two Socks was gone, he broke into a run.

Six mounted warriors streamed past him. They were raw, powerful men on painted, feathered horses. Their faces were streaked with colorful designs, their weapons slung around their shoulders. Dunbar kept running, barely aware of the aching in his legs, the quickness of his breathing. These were the Indians he had heard about, had dreamed about, had feared and been eager to meet. These were the wild Indians.

Their loud cries pierced the air. Helpless, Dunbar watched them rope Cisco and gallop away with him. Just when he thought they were gone, one stopped suddenly and turned to look back at Dunbar. Half the Indian's face was painted black, a stripe of yellow cutting across it; his hair flowed out behind him like a mane.

Wind In His Hair sat for a moment on his whirling pony, trying to decide if he should confront the white god, then made a warrior's choice. Shouting to the others to go on, he charged down the slope straight for Dunbar, his lance extended.

Dunbar lifted his revolver and held it out at arm's length.

Bringing his horse up quickly, the warrior shouted in Lakota, the tongue of the Sioux, "I am Wind In His Hair! Do you see that I am not afraid of you? Do you see?"

Unable to understand the words, Dunbar stared without expression into the Sioux warrior's eyes. He didn't blink. Secretly, he wondered if he was about to live his last, but outwardly he remained calm.

With a fearsome whoop, the Sioux

warrior turned sharply and rode off. The lieutenant watched him disappear. Then, taking a few steps in the direction of his quarters, he fell to the ground in a dead faint.

To confront his enemy as Wind In His Hair had done was a victory in the eyes of the Indians. To take his horse was another. But that part of his victory was short-lived, for Cisco was a horse who would not be so easily captured. He tore loose from the ropes that held him and was back at Fort Sedgewick by the time Lieutenant Dunbar regained consciousness.

In frustration, Wind In His Hair threw his lance to the ground. He was angry, but he also marveled at the white man's good fortune in owning such an animal. He remembered the soldier's coolness in the face of attack. Perhaps Kicking Bird was right. Perhaps this white man did have medicine.

✛ ✛ ✛

I realize I have been wrong, Dunbar wrote in his journal. *All this time I've been waiting. Waiting for what? For someone to find me? For Indians to take my horse? I am sick of it. I will ride out to the Indians. I've become a target. A target makes a poor impression. I am through waiting.*

✛ ✛ ✛

The next day, his boots and buttons polished, his uniform brushed, Dunbar mounted Cisco and set off to find the Indian camp. The Union flag fluttered from a staff stuck into one of his boots. He was determined to make a good impression.

After following the river for several miles, Dunbar's attention was caught by a strange sound. Not a bird, he thought, but a peculiar sort of singing. Reaching the top of a knoll, he saw a figure seated by a solitary cottonwood tree. It appeared to be the figure of an Indian woman. Her body was swaying; her voice chanted sadly.

On hearing hoofbeats, the woman turned. Dunbar was startled by her face and the color of her hair, neither of which seemed as much Indian as white. But he was even more surprised when the woman, clearly afraid, rose and turned to face him. Her dress was drenched in blood and a knife hung from her hand.

She began to move away.

"Wait," Dunbar called. "You need help. You're hurt."

Weak from the loss of blood, the woman fell. Dunbar dismounted and carefully approached her. "Let me help you," he said. But when he reached down to touch her, the woman screamed. "No!!"

He pulled back, but followed as the woman tried to crawl away.

"You're hurt," he said. And again, "You're hurt."

His face was filled with concern but the woman could not see it. All she saw

was a man who wore the skin and clothing of her enemy, a man who could not know that she had inflicted these wounds upon herself, cutting her own arms and

thighs as part of a sacred rite of mourning. No, it was not blood that frightened her, but the bloodless face of this pale white man. She must run, she must protect herself.

She raised the knife to strike him, but she was too weak. Dunbar lunged and grabbed her wrist, forcing her to drop the weapon. "Don't!" she screamed.

Dunbar was surprised, then confused. It was the second word of English he had heard the woman speak. But then she cried out, "Eoyo ma kipishneeka!"

"Don't come near me!" were her words. But because he did not understand and because he wanted to help her, he held her tight as she struggled against him until, overcome by fear and weakness, she threw back her head and wailed like a wolf.

And then she passed out.

Dunbar bound up her wounds as best he could. Her pony was nearby, but it was clear she couldn't ride by herself. He lifted her onto Cisco's back, mounted up behind, and continued riding slowly along the river to where the Indians were camped.

The first sight of the village spread out on the river's edge filled him with awe — the large pony herd, the smoke rising from the many fires, the tipis covered with well-used hides, the willow poles fanning against the sky. After all these weeks of being alone, Dunbar could hardly believe that a place so full of life had been so near.

He approached, and as he did several women gathered their children and ran for safety. Moments later, the entire village stood near the entrance

facing him, warriors at the front. Dunbar dismounted and, carrying the still unconscious woman in his arms, walked cautiously toward the others.

"She's hurt," he said.

Wind In His Hair stepped forward. "You are not welcome here," he said sharply. "Go away from us."

The lieutenant could not understand the Indian tongue. "No, she's hurt," he repeated.

Wind In His Hair knew the woman well. He tore her out of Dunbar's arms and dragged her limp body back to the camp. "Go away from us," he barked at the white man.

Without knowing the words, Dun-bar got the message and rode slowly away, puzzled and disappointed. Several warriors wanted to ride after him, but Kicking Bird held them back.

"The soldier did not come to fight," he told them. "He is going away and we will let him."

Though he reached Fort Sedgewick safely, Dunbar felt his mission had been a failure. He did not sleep well that night. He was haunted by his desire to communicate with the Indians, to let them know he meant them no harm.

And the face of the woman kept returning to his mind.

FINDING THE WORDS

The lieutenant was unprepared for the sight that greeted him the next morning. There, atop the bluff overlooking Fort Sedgewick, sat a line of warriors on horseback. Without taking his eyes off them, he reached for his rifle.

Two of the men saw this and began riding toward him. Wind In His Hair rode like a warrior, his face hard as a mask. He was not happy about coming to the soldier fort in peace; he was there only because Ten Bears had insisted. Kicking Bird, on the other hand, had readily accepted his chief's request that he lead a party to the white man to find out why he was at the fort. He saw this as an important moment in his life and the life of his people.

Dunbar could see that the two warriors were not approaching in a hostile manner. Putting down his weapon, he walked out to meet them. He recognized the faces of these two men at once. While he did not know their names he secretly called Kicking Bird the Quiet One and Wind In His Hair the Fierce One.

"Welcome," he said, beckoning nervously to the area in front of his sod hut. "Come. Please sit down."

Kicking Bird and Wind In His Hair could no more understand the white man's language than he could understand theirs, but they saw that he was trying to make them feel at home. They accepted his hospitality and dismounted.

Kicking Bird made the Sioux sign of greeting and the two Indians looked around the fort with great curiosity. They and Dunbar had no success in understanding each other, however, until the lieutenant decided to ask about the buffalo. In all the time he had been at the fort, he had not seen any and he was puzzled by their absence. For the Sioux, this absence was more than a puzzlement, it was a great worry. Without the buffalo, they would soon run out of food and would have difficulty surviving the long winter months.

Wind In His Hair watched with wide eyes as Dunbar wadded up his jacket

and bunched it up under his shirt, hoping it would indicate the buffalo's humped back. He then put his hands to his head like horns and snorted.

"His mind is gone," Wind In His Hair said matter-of-factly to Kicking Bird, and he started to rise.

But Kicking Bird motioned him to sit back down. He understood what the white man was trying to say.

"Tatanka."

Dunbar stopped immediately. "Tanka?" he said.

Kicking Bird repeated the Lakota word for buffalo. "Tatanka."

"Tatanka," Dunbar said. "Buffalo."

Kicking Bird watched the white man's lips intently. "B-buf ... buffalo."

The two men smiled at each other. It was a beginning.

The visits of Kicking Bird and Wind In His Hair continued and though communication built slowly, there was some progress. Dunbar began to learn a little sign language, and the Indians learned that this white man, while perhaps not a god, was also not their enemy.

Dunbar wrote in his journal, *The Fierce One, as I call him, seems a very tough fellow. I hope I never have to fight him. From what I know, he seems to be honest and direct. I like The Quiet One immensely. He's been patient and inquisitive. He seems eager to communicate. I would conclude that he is a man of some weight among his people.*

It wasn't long before the lieutenant convinced the warriors who waited each day for Kicking Bird and Wind In His Hair to come down from the ridge and join them.

One day, Dunbar entertained them by grinding coffee beans in a strange

wrote after that visit. He looked up from his journal and thought a moment about how hard communication continued to be. He thought of the look he had seen time and again in Kicking Bird's eyes.

So much goes unsaid. I feel these peo-

machine, then offered them fresh coffee. The taste didn't impress them until he supplied sugar to go with it. Seeing that a relationship was beginning to develop, he gave them coffee and sugar to take back with them to their village.

It's good to have some company, he

ple, particularly The Quiet One, want something from me.

✛ ✛ ✛

Kicking Bird, too, was frustrated by the slow pace of communication. He agreed with Ten Bears that a soldier who behaved as this one did was bound to be important among the whites. He was a man with whom agreements might be reached. Without agreements, war and suffering were sure to come. At the very least, he was someone who would know about the other white men who were coming. There were so many questions Kicking Bird needed to ask him. But first he needed the words with which to ask.

The medicine man thought hard before making his decision. He would call on the one resource he had not used before — Stands With A Fist, the woman the soldier had returned to the village after he had found her bleeding. She had been living with Kicking Bird and his wife in their tipi while she recovered. If she could be persuaded to remember the language she had spoken as a child, Kicking Bird would be able to speak to the soldier through her. He found Stands With A Fist and told her he needed to talk.

"Your wounds are healing well?" he asked. "You are happy here, with my family?"

She answered yes to both questions, but added, "I am missing my husband."

Kicking Bird nodded. Stands With A Fist was a young woman who had been married only a short time when her husband had been killed in battle with the Pawnee.

"Perhaps you will marry again when the time is right," he said.

"Perhaps." Stands With A Fist could see that Kicking Bird was leading up to something and she feared it. She kept her head bowed.

Kicking Bird began slowly. "We have word from many places that the whites are coming. They are coming into everyone's country."

Stands With A Fist raised her head and looked into the eyes of the

medicine man, waiting to hear more.

"I think they will soon be in ours. This white man who lives in the old soldier fort, I have visited him and I believe his heart is a good one."

"I am afraid of the white man at the fort," Stands With A Fist said. Her words began to flow like blood from a wound that would not be bound. "I am afraid he will tell others that I am here. I am afraid they will take me away. I've heard they take people away."

Kicking Bird looked deep into her eyes. "Every warrior in camp would fight them if they tried." He paused, then went on. "I cannot make the white man language. He cannot speak Sioux."

Stands With A Fist looked away nervously. "It has been a long time since I made the talk," she said.

"I want you to try."

"I can't," she told the medicine man. "It is dead in me."

Kicking Bird's eyes begged her to hear his words. "I do not ask this for myself. I ask this for all the people. Now, you must remember."

Stands With A Fist shook her head and began to sob. "I can't. I can't."

She ran out of the tipi, leaving Kicking Bird alone with his frustration.

✦ ✦ ✦

Stands With A Fist sat in the tall grass at the river's edge. She wanted to do as Kicking Bird asked, but the fear in her was great. It took a long time for her mind to open and let the past enter. The first words that rushed in were, "Run, Christine."

Her eyes were open and wet with the tears of remembering, but she no longer saw the light dancing on the water before her. Instead, she saw the scene from her girlhood, twenty summers earlier — that time when her life as a white child would end forever and her life as a Sioux would begin.

She was seven years old. Her family had just finished eating a picnic meal with neighbors. She and her friend Willie were lying on top of the sod roof

of their house when she spotted the Pawnee braves riding toward them. She couldn't remember what had started the argument, she couldn't hear the words. Perhaps the Pawnee wanted something her father would not give them. What she did remember was the tomahawk flying through the air. Her father fell. Her mother and the other grown-ups were trying to escape with the young children into the house. Willie cried, "Run, Christine." And she ran.

She hid for a long time in a dark hole in the side of a hill. It wasn't until the first light of the following day that the strong hands of a Sioux warrior pulled her out. She was afraid, but a young brave with a kind face helped her to be not afraid. His name was Kicking Bird.

He and his family looked after her, and in time she came to understand that these people were her people. Her memories dimmed and her new life began to be all she knew.

Stands With A Fist wiped the tears from her face. She would do as Kicking Bird asked of her. She would find her white tongue.

Dunbar was pleased by the invitation to visit the village on the river. Now that he had shared a pipe with Kicking Bird, however, he was not sure what to do next or, indeed, why he had been summoned in the first place. He was greatly surprised when the flap of the tipi was pulled back and through the opening stepped the woman he had found by the cottonwood tree. She looked much better than when he had first seen her and she was dressed as if for a special occasion. Kicking Bird turned to her immediately and spoke some words Dunbar did not understand.

Stands With A Fist looked at the lieutenant without expression and spoke with great effort. "H-hello. You … here … g-good."

The words were sweet music to Dunbar. He replied with a feeling of great relief.

"Thank you. I feel good."

Kicking Bird said in Lakota to Stands With A Fist, "Ask him why he is at the soldier fort."

"The s-s-soldier fort," Stands With A Fist began. "You come there—"

Dunbar jumped in before she could finish. There were things he had wanted to know for a long time. He asked what their names were and Kicking Bird agreed that introductions should come first. Slowly, searching her memory for the words and using signs when she could not remember, she pieced the Sioux names together for him. When Dunbar asked if Kicking Bird was a chief, she explained that he was a holy man.

Then the soldier introduced himself.

"Stands With A Fist," he said, "I am John Dunbar."

"Dunbar," she repeated.

Kicking Bird put his lips together in an effort to form these new sounds. "Dumb bear," he said.

The lieutenant laughed. "Not dumb bear," he said. "Dun-bar."

"Dunbar," Kicking Bird said.

"Dunbar," said Stands With A Fist.

✛ ✛ ✛

Back at Fort Sedgewick that night, Dunbar made an entry in his journal.

Nothing I've been told about these people is correct. They are not beggars and thieves. They are polite and have a familiar humor I enjoy. A woman among them speaks English and today progress was made.

Communication is slow, but one thing is clear. There are no buffalo, and it weighs heavily on their minds.

 **BUFFALO HUNT**

A rumbling like distant thunder woke Dunbar from his sleep. Dirt and dust fell from the roof over his head. Bottles began to clink, then tumble from the shelves and break on the floor. In a flash, the lieutenant knew that the thunder was not coming from the sky but from the earth itself.

Hastily, he lit a lantern and rushed out into the night. Walking along the bluff above the river, he stopped as a great wall of dust rose before him. There was something alive behind that wall of dust. The thunder was the sound of thousands of hoofbeats. It was the sound of the most powerful force on the prairie. The buffalo.

Within moments, Dunbar had mounted Cisco and the two were galloping along the river's edge to the Sioux camp, racing toward a great fire, where many of the band were gathered.

Men wearing buffalo headdresses

danced in the firelight. Dunbar pulled Cisco up in their midst, scattering the dancers. Cisco reared, and the lieutenant slid to the ground where he was immediately set upon by warriors, furious that this white man had interrupted their sacred dance. Kicking Bird pulled the warriors off Dunbar, scolding them angrily.

Out of breath, Dunbar said, "Buffalo! Buffalo!"

Kicking Bird knew this word. "Buffa ... Tatanka?"

"Tatankas," Dunbar repeated. "Tatankas. Yeah."

Kicking Bird turned to the crowd. "Tatanka!" he shouted. For a moment, there was silence. Then the Sioux exploded with excitement. Pulling Dunbar to his feet, they surged around him with yelps of joy.

The lieutenant was invited to join

the buffalo hunt the following day. By the time he returned from Fort Sedgewick, where he had gone to gather his things, the entire tribe was ready to move out. Spirits were high. Overnight the soldier had gone from a person of suspicion to one of genuine standing. He was greeted with open smiles and looks of appreciation.

One young Sioux, a boy named Smiles A Lot, seemed to take a special shine to the soldier, whom he called "Loo Ten Tant."

Scouts had picked up the buffalo's trail exactly where Dunbar had told them it would be. It was not difficult to find. A wide path of torn-up ground extended to the horizon. It was hard to imagine how many thousands of these beasts it had taken to create such an image.

Soon Dunbar made out a strange

Smiles A Lot

sight up ahead — a series of pink bumps on the ground with black specks all around them. At closer range, he saw that these were the remains of buffalo — buffalo that had been shot and stripped of their hides. The faces of the Indians as they rode past were full of sorrow and anger.

"Who would do such a thing?" Dunbar wondered to himself as they rode on. The field was proof enough that it was a people without values or soul, people who had no regard for Sioux rites.

The sight of wagon tracks sickened the lieutenant, for it confirmed what he already suspected. The killers could only have been white hunters.

Something had changed. Voices that had been joyous all morning were now as silent as the dead buffalo that had

been left to rot in this valley, killed only for their tongues and the price of their hides. Dunbar felt more deeply ashamed at that moment than he had ever felt in his life.

That night, when camp was pitched, he kept his distance from the others. Although he hadn't been made to feel unwelcome, neither did he know where he belonged. It was easiest to keep himself apart.

In the morning, however, Kicking Bird made sure that Dunbar was among those who followed the scouts to where the buffalo had been sighted. Leaving their horses at the bottom of a bluff, they clambered up the slope, dropping to their bellies as they neared the summit.

The line of men reached the crest together and peered over into an

immense valley. There were the buffalo, by the thousands, grazing quietly. Dunbar was overwhelmed by the scene. Once again, far from the life he had known, he felt as if he were living a dream.

Back at the camp, the horses' hides and the warriors' faces were painted with symbols in preparation for the hunt. Dunbar smiled at the bolts of yellow lightning Wind In His Hair painted on Cisco's flank. He was correct in thinking that this gesture on the Indian's part represented a great honor.

Soon the hunt began. The party of warriors advanced across the prairie, spreading out in a formation that would encircle part of the herd. Dunbar, rifle in hand, rode between Kicking Bird and Wind In His Hair. The Sioux were armed with bows and arrows. In the distance he could hear the low bellowing of the herd.

A sudden strike far ahead set the stampede in motion. Dunbar and Cisco hurtled over the prairie as pandemonium — or what felt like it to the inexperienced white man — broke loose. Dunbar smiled to himself at the thought that his buckskin seemed to know exactly what was expected of him while

he himself had no idea what to do but was doing it anyway.

The buffalo were very fast but Cisco was gaining with every stride. Dunbar raised his rifle at the blur of rumps and tails and flying hooves, almost lost in the clouds of dust everywhere. The sound was deafening.

He fired a wild shot, only grazing a buffalo's shoulder. Sioux hunters streamed past him, every man for himself, zeroing in on targets. The lieutenant heard the whiz of an arrow and watched as a buffalo tumbled to the ground, sending up a thick cloud of dust. He raised his gun again. Nothing in war had trained him for what he was now attempting to do. The speed, the sheer mass of his target, the smokescreen of dust made his task seem almost impossible. He marveled at the skill of his fellow hunters and vowed to make a kill. He aimed again and shot. The buffalo's front legs went out from under him. It was a hit.

On and on the hunters rode, choking on the dust, circling, sending their spears and arrows and bullets to strike, bringing down the buffalo.

Sitting atop his pony, the boy Smiles A Lot watched from the sidelines. He yearned for the day when he too would

was only yards from Smiles A Lot when a bullet pierced the beast's heart and it skidded to a halt at the boy's feet.

Lieutenant Dunbar rode up. "Are you all right?" he asked.

Dazed, Smiles A Lot nodded at the man who had saved his life.

The sounds of approaching riders turned Dunbar's attention in a different direction. The entire village was streaming onto the plains for the butchering. Wind In His Hair insisted that Dunbar take part in an age-old ritual of the kill. He sliced open the buffalo's belly, pulled out the still-warm liver and took a large bite of

join the hunt. Soon. It would be soon.

Without warning, a wounded bull veered from the stampede and charged straight at the young Sioux. Before Smiles A Lot could react, the buffalo hit his pony in the side and knocked them both to the ground.

Smiles A Lot scrambled to get back on his horse, but it was too late. The buffalo was set to charge again. The young boy could only watch in terror as the bull ran straight for him. He wanted to cry out, but fear and the need to be brave closed his throat and kept the cry inside.

A shot rang out in its place. Another and then another. The bull

As they were leaving one campfire on their way to another, the lieutenant noticed Wind In His Hair eyeing his army jacket. Without thinking, he took it off and offered it to the warrior. Delighted, Wind In His Hair removed the magnificent bone breastplate he wore and handed it to Dunbar.

"I can't," the lieutenant said. "This is too much."

it before offering it to the lieutenant. Dunbar could not refuse and with difficulty forced himself to take a second larger bite to show that he was one with his fellow hunters.

That night, there was great feasting around the fires, as warriors wandered from group to group, recounting their tales of the hunt. Dunbar made the rounds with Wind In His Hair, until he thought his stomach and his head would explode if he had to eat another bite or tell his story one more time. That he told his story without words, using his hands and his face and the mimicking sounds of buffalo hooves and gunfire only made his audiences enjoy it more. Their eyes grew teary with laughter, but there was something else in their eyes as well. Dunbar saw the message wherever he went: We accept you. You are one with us.

But he saw that Wind In His Hair was in earnest, and that his jacket gave the Indian as much pleasure as the Indian's breastplate gave him. And so, as Wind In His Hair put on the jacket, he placed the breastplate over his head and felt it come to rest.

"Good trade," he said. Wind In His Hair nodded.

After breaking camp the next day, the Sioux headed back to their home, dropping Lieutenant Dunbar off at Fort Sedgewick on their way. He watched them go, the sun setting behind them, and went inside to record the experiences of the past several days in his journal. He thought for a moment and then he wrote:

It seems every day ends with a miracle here.

◆◆◆◆◆◆◆◆◆ DANCES WITH WOLVES ◆◆◆◆◆◆◆◆◆

In the days that followed, Dunbar gave considerable thought to the changes that had occurred in his life. He wondered if the Great War in the east had ended. Perhaps the south had won. Was he even still a soldier in the United States Army, or were the United States now called The Confederate States of America? He realized he had been thinking less and less about the army. He was in the midst of a great adventure and he thought that it was possible he had stumbled on to a better life for himself. Cisco and Two Socks weren't human, but their loyalty was satisfying in ways that human relationships had never been.

And of course there were the Indians. He had been away from them for only two days, but it seemed much longer. He was drawn to these people; he felt comfortable with them. There was something wise about them, something that made him want to learn to see the world in the ways they did.

He determined that he would visit them the next day.

✛ ✛ ✛

Starting off for the village, the lieutenant looked very different from the day he had set out with his flag and polished buttons. Now his boots were worn and his trousers faded and he carried his rifle in the crook of his arm, Indian style.

After he had traveled some distance, he discovered that Two Socks was following him. Reining Cisco to a halt, he shouted at the old wolf, "Go home! Go home, Two Socks!" But when he tried

to move on, Two Socks trailed him like a shadow.

Finally, Dunbar got down off his horse and chased after his four-legged friend, scolding him. "Bad wolf!" he shouted. "Bad wolf!"

Two Socks thought this was a game. When Dunbar ran back to Cisco, the wolf ran after him, nipping him on the ankle and tripping him. The lieutenant looked up from where he had fallen, amazed at the wolf's playfulness.

In the distance, Kicking Bird and two other warriors watched these antics, both confused and impressed by a white man who danced with wolves.

Two Socks, alert to their presence, lifted his head and ran away. Brushing himself off, Dunbar went to meet the Indians who had been on their way to visit him at the fort.

✛ ✛ ✛

With this visit, the lieutenant began a new chapter in his life. Given a tipi of his own, he was made to feel at home and was encouraged to learn the language and the ways of his Sioux friends.

Kicking Bird was eager to find more words to build a bridge between the two of them. He asked Stands With A Fist not only to translate but to teach Dunbar the Lakota tongue.

On one of his rare visits back to Fort Sedgewick, Dunbar wrote in his journal, *We talk every day but Kicking Bird is frustrated with me. He always wants to know how many more white people are coming. I tell him that the*

white people will most likely pass through this country and nothing more. But I am speaking in half-truths. One day there will be too many, but I cannot bring myself to tell him.

On one occasion, the conversation between the white soldier and the Sioux medicine man turned to other things. A war party was going out against the Pawnee and Dunbar asked to go. He could see from the look on Kicking Bird's face that it may have been wrong of him to do so, but he couldn't take it back. The Sioux were his friends and the Pawnee had been very hard on them.

Kicking Bird did not reply right away. He wanted time to give thought to the soldier's request. When he was ready, he asked Stands With A Fist to translate.

"Kicking Bird wants to know why you want to make war on the Pawnee," she began. "They have done nothing to you."

"They are Sioux enemies."

Kicking Bird nodded and replied in Lakota.

Stands With A Fist translated his words. "Only Sioux warriors to go."

Dunbar felt his frustration growing. "Tell him that I have been a warrior longer than many of the young men who will go on this war party."

Stands With A Fist did so, then answered on Kicking Bird's behalf, "He says that the Sioux way of being a warrior is not the white way. You are not ready."

These were hard words for the lieutenant to hear. Kicking Bird had anticipated that they would be, and so he instructed Stands With A Fist to say, "He asks that you watch over his family while he is gone."

Dunbar turned to Kicking Bird, astonished, as Stands With A Fist added, "This thing he asks is a great honor."

The two men looked at each other with understanding and respect. "Tell him," Dunbar said, "that I would be happy to watch over his family."

After she told this to the medicine man, she turned to Dunbar and said, "He thanks Dances With Wolves."

The lieutenant looked confused. "Who is Dances With Wolves?"

"It is the name all the people are calling you now."

Dunbar thought, then remembered. "That's right. That day. How do you say it?"

Stands With A Fist replied, "Sung-manitutonka Ob Waci."

Dunbar repeated his new name in the Indian tongue and Kicking Bird smiled.

✛ ✛ ✛

At dawn the next day, a party of twenty warriors left to seek out the Pawnee. Kicking Bird and Wind In His Hair were among them. Dances With Wolves still wished he could go, but he took seriously his obligation to look after the medicine man's family. And he could not deny that he was looking forward to spending time with Stands With A Fist.

With little else to occupy his time, he enjoyed playing with the children, teaching them his games and learning theirs. Even more enjoyable were his lessons with Stands With A Fist. He was a good student, and a good-natured one even when he made mistakes. Stands With A Fist sometimes laughed at these, but the laughter was not unkind and Dances With Wolves found he enjoyed the sound of it almost as much as the words they spoke.

One day he asked, "How did you get your name?"

"I was not very old when I came to be with our people," she told him. "I was made to work. I worked very hard. There was one woman who didn't like me much. She used to call me bad names and sometimes she beat me. One day she was calling me these bad names with her face in my face and I hit her. I was not very big, but she fell down. And I stood over her with my fist and asked if there was any other woman who wanted to call me bad names.

"No one bothered me after that day."

Dances With Wolves grinned at her. "No, I wouldn't think so. Show me where you hit her."

Stands With A Fist made a fist and brushed him very gently at the point of his jaw. His eyes fluttered. They rolled up in his head and slowly he fell over backward. She slapped him lightly on either side of his cheeks, until he pretended to come back to life. They smiled shyly at their joke and at each other.

For a time, they did not speak. Then, Dances With Wolves asked, "Why are you not married?"

He could tell immediately this was not a good thing he had done. Stands With A Fist stopped smiling at once.

"I'm sorry," he said.

She stood and started away. "I have to go."

He offered to go with her, but she was hurrying away too quickly. He wondered what he had done wrong.

For the next few days, Dances With Wolves did not find Stands With A Fist where they were used to meeting. He was troubled, and sought out Stone Calf, one of the elders left behind in the village and a close friend of Ten Bears.

Dances With Wolves sat in the shade watching the old man paint a design on

a new buffalo-hide shield. After a time, he said, "I want to know about Stands With A Fist. Why is there no man with her?"

"She cries for someone," Stone Calf told him. "Her husband was killed not long ago. That is how you came to find her on the prairie."

Dances With Wolves nodded slowly. Now he understood why his question had caused Stands With A Fist pain. He knew he must give her time. And he needed time as well, time to think, time to be alone. He set off that day for a visit to Fort Sedgewick.

An old friend was waiting for him. Dances With Wolves crouched down and said, "Hello, Two Socks." Reaching into his vest pocket, he removed a pouch of dried meat and held a piece out at arm's length.

"Mmm?" he said to the wolf, smacking his lips.

He had never been able to get Two Socks to eat from his hand, but he had not given up trying either.

"You can do this," he reassured the wolf, who was getting up and slowly coming toward Dances With Wolves. He stopped about a foot away. "This is easy, Two Socks. You can do this."

Two Socks lowered his head and inched his way nervously toward the meat. Dances With Wolves never

looked away, but encouraged the old wolf with his eyes.

Suddenly, Two Socks lunged forward and snatched the meat away. Dances With Wolves laughed as he

watched the wolf run off to the bluff.

Inside the hut that had once been his home, he found his beloved journal lying on his bed. He smiled at the sketches he had drawn there, the words he had written. When he found his drawing of Stands With A Fist the way he had first seen her, sitting under the cottonwood tree, he was moved to pick up a pen and bottle of ink and make a new entry.

It would be his last.

I love Stands With A Fist, he wrote. And then he signed his name:

Dances With Wolves

ᐯᐯᐯᐯᐯᐯᐯ **FIGHTING THE PAWNEE** ᐯᐯᐯᐯᐯᐯᐯᐯ

Shortly after Dances With Wolves returned from the fort, word came that a party of forty or fifty Pawnee warriors was on its way to the Sioux village. Although the Pawnee frequently raided the large pony herds of the Sioux, this time they were not coming for horses. They were coming for blood.

"Hunters found them far to the north," Stone Calf told the others. "Soon they will be in our camp."

The most able warriors were still

away. How would the few who remained — mostly older warriors, women and children — defend themselves?

Dances With Wolves had an idea.

"I have many rifles," he told Stone Calf. "At the fort."

The older man shook his head. "No. The ride is long and we can spare no men."

"Guns would make one warrior like two," Dances With Wolves argued.

Stone Calf knew this to be true, and

though it was a risk, he agreed. "Take one man and go quickly."

Noticing the young Sioux standing nearby, Dances With Wolves said, "I will take Smiles A Lot."

By the time the two reached Fort Sedgewick, the weather had worsened and a sudden driving rain made it almost impossible to find the bone marker Dances With Wolves had placed in the ground where the weapons were buried. Just when they'd about given up hope, Smiles A Lot heard something snap under his pony's hoof. He jumped down to discover the bone, now broken in two. Calling to Dances With Wolves, he began digging in the mud until his hands hit the hard surface of a wood crate. Quickly, they pulled the boxes of weapons from the earth. No buried treasure could have pleased them more.

After their return to the camp, Dances With Wolves instructed the others in the use of the rifles. They were a small band and not the strongest, but they were armed. And they were ready.

Quiet as the morning fog rolling in, the first Pawnee came on moccasined feet. The horses in the Sioux herd lifted their heads at the change in the air. And then they ran, scattering everywhere, as the Pawnee warriors sneaked through them, using them as cover.

A war cry went up. The Pawnee set upon the village, tomahawks raised, the bloody taste of victory already on their tongues.

To their amazement, they were met by shots, the smoke of many rifles mingling with the fog, as the Sioux ran screaming down upon them. In a matter of seconds, many of the Pawnee lay dead.

As the battle raged, some of the Pawnee made their way to the lodges where the women and children hid. When a Pawnee warrior flung back the flap of Kicking Bird's tipi, the medicine man's wife shielded her screaming children in her arms. The Pawnee raised his hatchet to attack, but was stopped by a rifle's blast. As Stands With A Fist watched the Pawnee fall, she lowered the still smoking gun. At last, she had had revenge on her old enemies, the Pawnee — the same tribe that had killed her mother and father so long ago.

Most of the enemy were soon dead or making a retreat as fast as they could. Dances With Wolves spotted one warrior racing away down the river. This was the toughest-looking of them all and Dances With Wolves suspected he was their leader. He spurred Cisco on and charged after him.

Other Sioux moved to block the fleeing warrior's retreat. Soon he was surrounded. The circle slowly tightened as he wheeled his pony in the center, trying to find an opening through which to escape. When he saw that it was hopeless, he threw his war club high in the air and let loose a last defiant scream as many rifles spoke as one.

All at once the battle was over. The Pawnee attackers lay where they had fallen. Some of the Sioux had been wounded or killed, too. Sadly, Dances With Wolves saw now that Stone Calf was among the dead.

As he watched Ten Bears cradle the body of his old friend in

his arms, he heard his own name being chanted by the other warriors who had gathered around thanking him for his part in the victory. He thought how

different this battle had been from any he'd ever fought in a war. He had not been fighting for some political ideal or territorial boundary; instead, he fought to protect family and keep the food supply safe for the winter. This kind of fighting made sense to him and filled him with pride. It struck him that he had never known who Lieutenant John Dunbar was. Perhaps the name had no meaning. But this new name, this Dances With Wolves ... for the first time, he knew who he really was.

✦ ✦ ✦

Peace returned to the village and Dances With Wolves resumed his lessons and talks with Stands With A Fist. The more time they spent together, the more he felt his love for her grow. He could see in her eyes — and the way she lowered them sometimes when he held his gaze on her a moment too long — that she had feelings for him as well.

Stands With A Fist had known for some time that she was ready to put her mourning behind her. Her heart had opened to this man she'd once feared and she was certain that they could be one.

In time, she no longer lowered her eyes when he gazed at her but held his look, and their love was sealed, an unspoken agreement between them.

When the war party led by Kicking Bird and Wind In His Hair returned to the village in victory, Kicking Bird and his wife, Black Shawl, had a talk about Stands With A Fist.

"She has found love again," Black Shawl informed her husband.

"With — ?"

"Dances With Wolves."

Kicking Bird was surprised. "Are you certain of this?"

"When you see them together, you will know."

"What are people saying?"

"They like the match."

"No one is angry?" the medicine man asked. Black Shawl shook her head. "It makes sense," she told him. "They

are both white."

Kicking Bird nodded. He knew it was up to him to free Stands With A Fist from her time of mourning and to give his blessing to her union with Dances With Wolves. After all, he was her only father in this world.

And so the match was made and a wedding day set.

The entire village was there. Kicking Bird greeted Dances With Wolves. "This is a good day for me," he said.

"And for me," Dances With Wolves answered.

He looked at Stands With A Fist then, her beauty like the prairie and the blue sky and the setting of a thousand suns, and he prayed that he would live to an old age because he knew he would never tire of looking at her.

LIKE THE STARS

The chill of the coming winter was in the air.

One day shortly before the band was due to move to their winter camp, Kicking Bird asked Dances With Wolves to ride with him. Most often when the medicine man rode out of the camp, he rode alone. He liked time to think, to be with the Great Spirit who was everywhere, in every living thing. But on this day he wanted Dances With Wolves for company. And he wanted to talk.

Dances With Wolves sensed this, but neither he nor Kicking Bird spoke for some time. When they stopped to rest their horses, Kicking Bird looked at his friend for a long time. It was hard to believe that this white man who had never seen an Indian only a few months before was now a Sioux.

"I was just thinking," Kicking Bird said, "that of all the trails in this life, there is one that matters most. It is the trail of a true human being. I think you are on this trail, and it is good to see."

These words pleased Dances With Wolves. He took them in and kept them in his heart.

Now he knew it was time to answer the question that had hung so long between him and Kicking Bird.

"You always ask about the white people," he said haltingly. "You always want to know how many more are coming." He stopped and turned away. "There will be a lot, my friend, more than can be counted."

"How many?" Kicking Bird asked.

Dances With Wolves looked back at the medicine man. "Like the stars," he told him. "It makes me afraid for all the Sioux."

Kicking Bird stared down at the ground, his heart crying.

"We should tell this to Ten Bears," he said.

✦ ✦ ✦

When they got back to camp, they went immediately to the chief's tipi to talk about what Dances With Wolves had told Kicking Bird. For a long time, the old man puffed away on his pipe in silence. Then he got up and took down a bundle, which he brought back to the fire and slowly unwrapped. Dances With Wolves recognized the rusted hulk of metal from pictures he had seen. It was the helmet of a conquistador, one of the warriors from Spain who had come long ago to conquer this land.

Ten Bears held the helmet in both his hands as he spoke.

"The men who wore this came in the time of my grandfather's grandfather," he told them. "Eventually we drove them out. Then the Mexicans came. They do not come here anymore. In my own time, the Texans have been here like all the others. They take without asking."

He looked up at Dances With Wolves. "I don't know if we are ready for these people. But I think you are right. I think they will keep coming. When I think of that, I look at this helmet. Our country is all that we have and we will fight to keep it."

Dances With Wolves nodded. He

knew that the white men who were coming now were not like those who had come before. They were many and they were strong and they would let nothing come between them and what they wanted.

All day, Ten Bears' words returned to him. Just before entering his tipi for sleep, he walked away from the camp and gazed out at the vast prairie. In his mind, he saw the chief's face and heard his voice, as old as time:

"Our country is all that we have."

When they broke camp the next morning, Dances With Wolves was relieved that they would be going far away to where they would live for the winter. He and Stands With A Fist were hoping to have a child soon and it troubled him to be so near the fort of the white soldiers.

When Stands With A Fist asked him if he had everything he needed from that place, he replied, "Yes. There's nothing for me there."

But then he remembered. He had left his journal on the cot in his old quarters.

"The book is like a trail for people to follow," he told Kicking Bird. "It tells everything about my life here. I must get it."

Kicking Bird understood, but he explained that they could not delay their leaving to wait for his return. "I'll catch up," Dances With Wolves told him. Turning to Stands With A Fist, he said again, "I'll catch up."

With tears in her eyes, Stands With A Fist watched him mount Cisco and ride off.

+ + +

Cisco was happy to be racing across the prairie, the crisp, autumn wind in his face. They breezed over the miles to the fort. The last familiar rise loomed ahead of them, and Dances With Wolves flattened down on his horse's back, asking him to take the final half mile at a full run.

They blew over the rise and shot down the slope to the old post. When alarm: "Injun! Get him! Injun!"

The soldiers opened fire. Cisco reared up, while Dances With Wolves tried to bring him under control.

"Keep firin'!" a voice shouted.

More shots rang out and Dances With Wolves felt Cisco snap under him. "No!" he cried, just as Cisco fell heavily, throwing him to the ground. When his head cleared, he crawled to Cisco, holding him in his arms and comforting

Dances With Wolves saw what lay ahead, it was too late to turn back.

The fort swarmed with soldiers. There were as many as fifty bluecoats going about their tasks, including a group in a wagon close by. In a heartbeat, they had seen him and scrambled for their guns, screaming out the him as he lay dying.

He turned at the sound of footsteps. Soldiers were advancing from every direction, their rifles aimed at his head, their trigger fingers tense and ready.

All he could think was, "It's over."

◆◇◆◇◆ PRISONER AT THE SOLDIER FORT ◇◆◇◆◇

Kicking Bird looked up at the sun. The day was more than half over. "Something has happened," he said. "Dances With Wolves is not coming."

Wind In His Hair knew in his heart that the medicine man's words were true. "He must have trouble."

Kicking Bird nodded and said, "Pick two good men and send them back to the soldier fort."

As Wind In His Hair rode away, Kicking Bird again scanned the horizon. In seeing nothing, he saw everything. Dances With Wolves was not coming.

✛ ✛ ✛

His head ached from where he had been hit by a rifle butt moments after the soldiers had surrounded him. Now he lay in handcuffs in the hut he had once singlehandedly filled with supplies. The soldier who guarded him spat on the floor and shouted to someone outside that the prisoner was conscious. Another soldier, an officer, came in to question him.

The officer looked long and hard at Dances With Wolves. Nobody had been able to figure this prisoner out. Was he white or was he an Indian?

"You speak English? Talk!"

Reluctantly, Dances With Wolves used his white tongue. "I speak English."

"Who are you?"

"Lieutenant John J. Dunbar. This is my post."

"Why are you dressed like that?"

Dances With Wolves avoided the question. "I came out from Fort Hays last April, but nobody was here."

Another officer piped up. "You have proof of that?"

Nodding, Dances With Wolves said, "My journal's in my quarters. My orders are in the journal. It'll tell you everything."

The officers exchanged a look, then turned to one of the men guarding the prisoner. "Spivey, you and Edwards were the first ones here. Did you find anything? A journal?"

The private, an oily man with the look of a bully, shrugged. "We didn't find nothin', sir."

Dances With Wolves raised his head. What could have happened to his journal? He saw now the officers didn't believe him.

"What is the army doing out here?" he asked.

"We are charged with arresting hostile Indians, recovering stolen property, getting back white captives taken in raids."

"There are no hostile Indians here," said Dances With Wolves.

The officer snorted. "We'll be the judge of that." Then, staring hard at the white man in the Indian clothes, a thought occurred to him. "If you guide us to these camps, your conduct will be reevaluated. Your status as a traitor might improve should you choose to cooperate with the United States Army."

Dances With Wolves closed his eyes in pain. He would not betray his fellow Sioux — even if it meant death.

"Are you willing to cooperate or not? Speak up!"

"Sungmanitutonka Ob Waci miye. I am Dances With Wolves."

"What's that?"

"Nitaku ni pi sni yelo. I have nothing to say to you."

The officer frowned. "Take this man to the river," he said, his voice full of contempt and pity. "Let him clean up his face."

For a moment, Private Spivey was alone. He pulled a book out of his jacket and looked through its pages. He could not read so he did not know what the writing said. Maybe it was the journal everyone was talking about. But he was afraid if he turned it in he might be charged with theft. Besides, toilet paper was scarce here and that was the reason he'd taken it in the first place. Better to leave it hidden. He tucked it back inside his jacket.

Dances With Wolves, meanwhile, washed his face at the river as best as he could while mannacled in handcuffs. He did not know that his actions were being observed. High up on the bluff above the river, two Sioux scouts watched in silence. Dismayed by what they saw, they ducked down below the

ridge and rode off to report to Wind In His Hair and Kicking Bird.

The commanding officer was watching Dances With Wolves, too. He did not like the idea of keeping this difficult soldier around. It seemed he had "turned Injun" and would rather die than cooperate. After some thought, the officer decided the best plan would be to send the prisoner back to headquarters at Fort Hays. That way, he would be rid of a nuisance and get credit for capturing a "hostile" at the same time. Spivey took special pleasure in this news. He would be one of the escorts, which meant a chance to get away from the fort and out in the open. Besides, he wanted to see this dirty traitor get his just deserts.

"They're gonna ship you back to Hays," he told Dances With Wolves when no one else was around. "And once you get there … they gonna hang you." Grinning widely, he kicked at Dances With Wolves' bound ankles.

On the morning the wagon began its trek to Fort Hays, Wind In His Hair was readying a party of six warriors to ride to the fort and capture Dances With Wolves. Smiles A Lot begged to go with them and Wind In His Hair agreed, but he made it clear that the boy was only coming to hold the horses when the attack took place.

As the soldiers and their prisoner made their way across the river and over the open prairies he so loved, Dances With Wolves looked up from where he sat on the wagon's bed. Spivey looked down with a sneer.

Dances With Wolves felt his hatred of the private burn in his innards like the hottest coal in the heart of a fire. The man was stupid and cruel, and he seemed to take special pleasure in tormenting his prisoner. The other private — Edwards, his name was — was almost as bad. Dances With Wolves had forgotten there were men like these in the world.

He did not give up hope that his Sioux brothers would come for him. From time to time, he gazed up at a ridge in the distance for any sign of riders.

However, the first living creature anyone saw once they'd left the fort was not an Indian but a wolf.

"Hey, what is that?" Dances With Wolves heard one of the soldiers say.

He looked up to see Two Socks following the wagon at a distance. In horror, he watched the soldiers raise their rifles and take pot shots at his old companion. Sadly, he realized that because of their friendship, Two Socks had lost his instinct to run. He was no longer afraid of men — even when he should be.

The soldiers quickly made a game out of the slowly moving target.

"You missed him."

"Don't shoot. It's my shot."

"Hey, wait. I seen him first."

"Get him. He's standin' there."

Unable to take it anymore, Dances With Wolves kicked Spivey's feet out from under him, spoiling his shot. In his rage, he wrapped his ankles around the private's neck. It took all the other men and a blow to Dances With Wolves' head to free Spivey.

"He might've killed you," one of the men said. Spivey glared at Dances With Wolves as if to say, I'd like to kill *you*. He retrieved his gun then and returned to the game.

Two Socks was darting back and forth across the field, more confused than afraid. "Run," Dances With Wolves thought. "Run away!"

But Two Socks would not run, and finally one of the soldier's bullets found its mark. "I got him!" the soldier shouted. Dances With Wolves squeezed his eyes shut as the soldier shouted again, "I got him!"

✛ ✛ ✛

The wagon was crossing the river when the Sioux struck. One of the two soldiers riding in advance received the first arrow. The other was the next to go. The shots were clean and true; neither man had time to know he was about to die.

The same could not be said of the men in the wagon. Their hearts froze with fear as they heard the terrible war cries and saw the painted faces of Wind In His Hair and the other warriors charging toward them. They raised their rifles, but the Sioux were too quick for their bullets.

Several of the men jumped into the river in an effort to escape. Dances

With Wolves jumped in after one of them. Grabbing the scarf from around Spivey's neck, he twisted it until the private was gasping for breath. He then pushed his former tormentor's head under the water and held it there until the gasping stopped.

In a matter of minutes, there was only one soldier left alive. In the confusion of the battle, he made his way to the cover of weeds along the riverbank. Crashing through the thicket, he came to a clearing where he found himself face to face with Smiles A Lot, who had been left to guard the horses.

The soldier, seeing the horses as his means of escape, aimed his revolver at the startled boy and pulled the trigger. But the hammer only clicked; there were no bullets left in the gun. He struck Smiles A Lot then and grabbed for one of the ponies when a bone-chilling whoop stopped him cold. Terrified by the sound, he turned to see Wind In

His Hair coming at him with full force.

The soldier began to run. He hadn't gotten far when a hatchet caught him in the back. The pain was intense, but before he died he wanted to look into the face of the man who killed him.

What he saw when he turned was not a man's face. It was a boy's. As the soldier dropped, Wind In His Hair rode up beside Smiles A Lot and whooped his approval of the boy's first kill.

To the warrior's surprise, Smiles A Lot just walked away without a word. The young Sioux sat down on the shore of the river and buried his head in his arms. He knew he should be glad for what he had just done, but inside him was a big empty space and sadness was the only thing that would fill it.

Like a violent storm in summer, the battle had raged and was over. The Indians searched the bodies of the soldiers. It didn't take long to find the keys that would unlock the handcuffs still binding Dances With Wolves' hands. In his looking, one of the warriors found something in the pocket of Spivey's jacket, but thinking it wasn't anything useful, he tossed it aside.

Gently, Lieutenant John J. Dunbar's journal floated away on the river's current.

The winter camp was nestled in a steep-walled canyon in the mountains, well-hidden and sheltered from the prairie winds. There was plenty of wood for fires, and the buffalo hunts of the previous summer had supplied Ten Bears' band with enough meat to last through the season.

With the success of the rescue party and Dances With Wolves' return, the general feeling among the band was one of well-being and security. But these feelings were not shared by Dances With Wolves. He was deeply troubled.

Finally, he asked that Ten Bears call a meeting of the council.

As was the custom, the peace pipe was shared before any words were exchanged. Ten Bears could see the unhappiness in Dances With Wolves' face. At last, he spoke.

"Dances With Wolves is quiet these days," he said. "Is his heart bad?"

Dances With Wolves did not answer right away. He wanted to choose his words carefully.

"Killing the soldiers at the river was a good thing," he began. "I was glad to do it."

Several of the council members mur-

murred their assent.

"But the soldiers hate me now, like they hate no other. They think I am a traitor and they will hunt for me."

He fell silent. He could not bring himself to say, I am a traitor in the white men's eyes because I have chosen to live among you.

"When they find me, they find you," he said. "I think it would be wise to move the village now." He then spoke words that cut through his heart like an arrow.

"I will be leaving."

A cry of protest rose up from the council. Wind In His Hair jumped up and shouted angrily at Dances With Wolves.

Ten Bears raised his hand. "Quiet. You are hurting my ears." He ordered the council members to leave him alone with Dances With Wolves.

After the others had gone, Ten Bears put his peace pipe down by the fire. "You are the only white man I have ever known," he told Dances With Wolves. "I have thought about you a lot. More than you know. But I think you are wrong. The man the soldiers are looking for no longer exists. Now there is only a Sioux named Dances With Wolves."

He picked up the pipe and said, "Let's smoke awhile."

Dances With Wolves accepted the pipe. He listened to Ten

Bears talk of simple pleasures. He knew that the old man was trying in his own way to convince him to stay. But he also knew he was a danger to them now. He must leave as soon as the snow broke. He would go to find white people who would listen to him. Surely there would be people somewhere who were not afraid to hear the truth about the Indians.

✛ ✛ ✛

When Dances With Wolves told Stands With A Fist his decision, she did not speak at first.

"You have nothing to say?" Dances With Wolves asked.

"My place is with you," she said at last. "I go where you go."

"You're not afraid?"

"No." She was sad, but she did not

have to tell her husband that. She
could feel the sadness in his body, too.
It was something unspoken they
shared, like their love.

"Have you told everyone?" she asked.

Dances With Wolves thought for a
moment. "Not everyone," he said.

Wrapping his buffalo robe around
him, he set off in search of Kicking
Bird. He carried the pipe he had been
making as a parting gift for his friend.
When he recognized the medicine man
coming toward him on the path that
ran through the village, he saw that he
too was carrying a pipe.

They stopped and acknowledged
each other with a nod. "You, uh … finish your pipe?" Kicking Bird asked,
groping for the words in English.

Dances With Wolves handed it to
him. "Good pipe," Kicking Bird said,
admiring it. "How does it smoke?"

Dances With Wolves smiled. He had
just finished making it. "I've never
smoked it," he said.

Kicking Bird handed him the pipe he
had brought with him. "We come far,

you and me," he said. Accepting the
gift, Dances With Wolves said, "I will
not forget you."

The two men had no more words.
They looked into each other's faces, let-
ting their eyes speak for their hearts.

On his way back to his tipi, Dances
With Wolves was approached by Smiles
A Lot. The boy held out a gift wrapped
in animal skin which Dances With
Wolves opened in puzzlement. He was
stunned to discover his water-stained
journal, which the boy had spied float-
ing by and fished out of the river the
day of the rescue. Dances with Wolves
thanked Smiles A Lot, then turned to
continue on his way.

In the few days it took them to get
ready to leave, Dances With Wolves
and Stands With A Fist said goodbye to
everyone except Wind In His Hair.
Now, on the morning of their depar-
ture, the warrior was not to be found.

His absence saddened them, but the
cold, harsh wind told them they must
begin on their journey. Turning to take
one last look at the village, they saw

men and women and children going about their tasks, but the air, usually filled with talking and laughter and song, was now heavy with silence.

As the couple rode up the trail that would take them away from the camp, a plaintive cry echoed through the canyon. High on a ledge near the canyon rim, Wind In His Hair sat on his pony, his lance raised. He called out in his Indian tongue the words he could not deliver in person.

"Dances With Wolves, Dances With Wolves. I am Wind In His Hair. Do you see that I am your friend? Can you see that you will always be my friend?"

The wind carried these words to Dances With Wolves and the sound of them died with the wind. But the words themselves were locked forever in Dances With Wolves' heart. No matter what happened to him now, every-thing, everything he had known and felt and heard in the time he had lived with Ten Bears' band would be locked in his heart forever. No one would be able to take these things from him, for he alone possessed the key.

✝ ✝ ✝

By the time the army troops reached the site of Ten Bears' camp, the chief and his people were long gone. They had covered their tracks well; even with the help of Pawnee scouts, the sol-diers were unable to find them. As they turned back in defeat, a wolf howled somewhere in the canyon.

Far away, Dances With Wolves and Stands With A Fist heard it, too. They stopped for a moment and listened. Then they continued on their way up the steep mountainside into the win-tery night.

The winter snows melted and the spring rivers flowed. Ten Bears and his band returned to their summer camping grounds. And somewhere, in another part of that land, Dances With Wolves and Stands With A Fist prepared for the birth of their first child. It was a bountiful summer. The earth was giving and the buffalo ran free. The yellow prairie met the blue sky in four directions and there was peace.

But the coming of the white man was a force greater than the Indians had ever known. It did not thunder like buffalo hooves; it did not blind like the sun. But it overcame them with a power neither the buffalo nor the sun possessed, robbing them of food and shelter, of their land and their freedom.

In 1877, the last band of free Sioux submitted to white authority at Fort Robinson, Nebraska. From that day forward, the Indians lived where the white men told them to. Outwardly, their spirit was broken. But all that they knew, all that they would pass on to the next generation and the next, this was locked in their hearts.

And this could not be taken from them because only they possessed the key. ✝